The Gospel of Joe

Journey with the

greatest "man" that ever lived

www.gospelofjoe.com

ISBN: 979-8-218-97769-6

CONTENTS

Power

The greatest "man" who ever lived was executed at age 33. And yet his teachings and message have outlived empires and will continue to do so.

Whatever your beliefs, this book offers you a way to better understand him.

1. POWER

Power to Save

[an excerpt from a discussion between Joe and the US President, from later in the story]

"Who are you, really? Where are you from, exactly?" The President asked Joe many questions, but Joe stayed quiet.
"Joe, why aren't you defending yourself?"
Joe remained silent.
"Talk to me. Let me help you. Give me something," the President urged. "These are serious accusations. Don't you get it? I can save your life."
"No, you can't," Joe replied. "Your power comes from your position, and that authority is given from above. The real guilt lies with those who have conspired to kill me."

I'm Not Ready

"I'm not ready yet."
But Joe's mother ignored his protests and asked the festival staff to listen to his instructions.
"Mom, this isn't my problem. And I'm not ready to start my campaign. What do you expect from me?"

Right at the beginning, when our team had just started volunteering with Joe, we went to a local music festival that had run out of beer halfway through the afternoon. At his mother's insistence, Joe instructed the staff to fill kegs with water and begin serving it to the customers. Out of the kegs flowed beer of such high quality that everyone raved about it.

This was the first time we had seen anything like this. Joe's mother explained that there had always been something special about him, and that at a young age he understood theology to such a degree that he taught the local church leaders. Many had predicted that he would be a great leader with some even prophesying this before he was born.

When the news spread of what had happened at the festival, it ignited both excitement and confusion, launching our campaign into the public's attention.

The Senator's Son

A senator had heard the rumors about Joe and came to see him about his terminally ill son.

While the senator was explaining his son's cancer diagnosis and treatments, Joe interrupted, "People always want proof. They're always looking for miracles."
The senator begged, "Please, just come to my home and see my son."
"No need. He's already been cured."

Test results taken that later day confirmed that his son's cancer had completely disappeared. From that day onward, the senator and his entire family became vocal supporters of Joe.

Going Viral

Joe was fast becoming a celebrity. When he was recognized in public places, crowds gathered around him in minutes. People came to him for help and advice, so he spent hours listening, and dealing with their pain. Not only did people with mental health problems get relief, but paraplegics began to walk again, blind people regained their sight, and deaf people regained their hearing. While he treated them, he spoke to everyone about the great hope he had for the country.

These events went viral on social media where he was both loved and attacked. The mainstream media began to do their utmost to discredit and cancel him.

Prove It

"If you are as powerful as you claim, prove it to me. Turn these stones into bread."

Joe took some time out and camped alone in the high desert for weeks, fasting, praying, and waiting. His rival had also been waiting, waiting for a moment of weakness to tempt Joe away from his mission. Joe responded with a verse from the Bible explaining that life is more than just physical. "We need God. Our life depends on God's truth."

His rival took him to nearby cliff and provoked him, "If you depend on God, prove it. Jump off and let Him save you."
"You cannot trick God and put him to the test."

Joe's rival then took him up in a private jet and showed him the great cities across the state.

"I will give you control of everything. Not just California but also power over the entire country. I can make you the most powerful man on earth. Think about what you could do with that power. All you need to do is show loyalty to me."

Considering what was at stake, Joe answered "I can only be devoted to one master. And it will never be you."

Joe's rival decided to wait for another moment of weakness to try again.

Jealousy

Joe was later invited to speak at the church where he grew up. He began by reading a key verse from the Old Testament, from the book of Psalms, which says, "God's power is with me because I was born for this purpose: to bring the good news of God to the poor, to speak about freedom for prisoners, to give sight to the blind, to liberate people from oppression and to announce the new era in which God will cancel every debt."

As Joe read the passage, the people fell silent in anticipation. Joe concluded by saying, "This passage is speaking about me!"

This immediately provoked anger in the church. "Who are you to claim this? You're nobody! You're a mechanic! You are not a saint or some prophet! You are deceiving yourself and misleading others. You cannot be the chosen one of God. That is blasphemy!" "I know what you want. You want proof. You want me to perform a miracle here, right now, at your convenience. But why do you need proof to believe?"

The shouting made it hard to hear Joe. "I will not perform a miracle for you! Because great leaders are never respected in their hometown. They travel the world and gain fame for the things they achieve - but those at home are filled with jealousy. You are just the same. You have no faith!"

This set off a small mob who tried to attack Joe, but he managed to escape.

Death is Not the End

A year later, Joe was executed, accused of leading a terrorist group aiming to overthrow the government through a violent insurrection. Fortunately, for all of us, his death is not the end.

2. FORGIVENESS

Forgiveness, Not Sacrifice

Max was a former Mayor of LA, infamous for his tax increases and corruption. Joe asked Max to join our team and host a fundraiser with his wealthy and notorious friends.

Social media blew up with criticism of Joe, to which he responded, "Healthy people don't need a doctor, but those in pain do. Go and learn what this means: 'I desire forgiveness, not sacrifice.' I'm not here to lead the righteous. I'm here for those who want to change."

Authority to Forgive

We were visiting a friend when word got out that Joe

was around. Hundreds of people from the neighborhood came over to see and hear him speak.

Friends of a paralyzed woman in that neighborhood wanted to bring her to Joe but the crowd was blocking the front door. So, they went around the back of the house, broke a window, and lifted her wheelchair through. This caught Joe's attention, and they made space for her in front of him.

Joe told her, "I forgive all your mistakes and failures."

Some local church leaders who were nearby protested, saying it was blasphemous because only God can forgive people. Joe responded, "I have a question for the biblical experts here. What's easier? To say she's forgiven or to cure her paralysis?"

The room fell silent as Joe waited for an answer. "Let me make this crystal clear. I have the authority on earth to forgive!" Then Joe spoke to the woman, "Stand up and walk out of here."

She gripped the wheelchair and lifted herself carefully onto her rapidly strengthening legs. She took a few small steps, gained confidence, and walked right out of the house while everyone erupted in cheers and tears because they had never seen anything like it before.

Unexpected Faith

Joe's popularity continued to grow at the same rate as the opposition to his campaign.

He performed another miracle where a CEO asked us to help an employee who had been paralyzed in a terrible accident. Joe offered to go and see the employee in the hospital, but the CEO refused, explaining, "Just give the order, and it will be done. I'm an employee hired by my board to run the company. Based on that authority, I can instruct my employees to get things done. You only need to exercise your authority, and it will be done."

Joe was really surprised by the CEO's answer. "I haven't seen this much faith in anyone at church. It shows that many unchurched people will join God's party, while many churchgoers might not be invited."

At that exact time, the paralyzed employee got up from his hospital bed and ran about the room. These events fueled the fiery debate around Joe's identity and his ambitions.

Alternative Energy

One day we stopped off at a gas station to fill up and get some food. Joe waited outside and asked a woman if she could fill up our van too.

"Mister, I barely have enough money to get through the week. I'm sorry but I can't help you", she replied.
""If you knew God's gifts, you'd be asking me for something better than gas. You would ask me for an infinite source of energy."
"I don't understand. Where can I get this energy?"
"It doesn't work like you expect," replied Joe. "Your car needs filling up again and again. But the energy I am offering you will never run out."
"Okay. So, what must I do to get it?"
Joe answered, "Call you husband and ask him to come here."
"Well... I'm not really married." she said.
"True. You have had been married five times. And now you are living with some other guy."
"How do you know that?!"
"I know everything about you" Joe replied.
"Who are you? Are you an angel or something? I pray but I'm not religious."
"You pray to something you don't understand. At least Christians follow something that they understand will save them. But what God really wants is people to give their heart and soul to him completely."
She asked, "I have heard there is a man of God who is doing some crazy things around here recently. People say he is promising us a better way of life."
"They are talking about me", Joe answered.

We didn't want to disturb Joe's conversation with the woman, so we had no idea what they were talking

about.
As we drove off, Joe said, "I have food that you guys don't understand."
"Did you go to Burger King while we were inside?" someone joked.
Joe continued, "The food I'm talking about is the nourishment I get from doing my job, which is the work God has given me to do."

He continued, "One hears the advice, 'Don't sell your investments too early because they will pay off in the long term.' But you don't realize that the time has come to sell, and many people are already cashing in. You guys need to wake up! You can cash in on investments made by others. They have done the hard work, but you will earn the profits."

The woman at the gas station told all her friends and family about Joe, how he already knew everything about her, and about the amazing gift he had offered. She invited us to stay with her for a couple of days, during which time, practically the whole neighborhood became passionate followers of Joe.

3. TEACHINGS

The Sermon on YouTube

We produced a series of short videos on YouTube to reach more people. They went viral, as people all over the world engaged with Joe's unique teachings. The comments were filled with speculation over where Joe studied or who influenced him as they tried to explain how he was able to teach with such clarity and power.

The next sections are an overview of the lessons.

True Happiness

"If you are searching for heaven on earth, for a meaningful life and true happiness, then understand this:

It starts by accepting that you need God. It begins with grief. It has its origin in humility. It has its foundation in hunger for justice and compassion for others. It grows from pure motives and dedication to peace.

If people criticize or attack you for living in this way, celebrate it! The rewards waiting for you will be even greater because you stayed true.

However, those who are rich have already received their comfort. Those that are well fed will go hungry and those who are laughing now will grieve. If everyone speaks well of you, then you had better think twice.

Purpose

I want you to be like refrigerators. Your purpose in this world is to prevent things from going bad. If a fridge stops working and can't keep food from going bad, the fridge is useless and gets thrown away.

I want you to be like billboards along a highway where everyone can see them. The good things you do will be seen by those on their journey and it will bring honor to God.

Anger

The law states that murder is a crime. But you are already guilty if you store anger for others in your heart, when you speak harshly against them. Instead, if you have a grudge against someone, go and forgive them before you approach God.

Always try to settle matters with your adversaries out of court. Up until the last moment, look for a way to settle because you never know how it'll turn out in court.

Lust

We know it is wrong to sleep with someone else's partner. But you are already guilty when you entertain such thoughts.

If you can't find a way to control your thoughts, it would be better to blind yourself so that your soul is saved.

Divorce

Divorce is taken very lightly these days, but if you get divorced for reasons other than cheating, you're in serious danger. If you divorce your spouse and they marry someone else, you will make them a victim of adultery in God's eyes.

Judging Others

When you judge someone, you create a standard that other people will use to judge you. And how can you be sure whether your judgment is sound? You are like a person that points out a small speck of dirt on your friend's sunglasses. But you don't see that your own glasses are covered in dirt. Clean your own glasses before inspecting the cleanliness of others.

Revenge

In the law they speak about proportionality, where the punishment should fit the severity of the crime. But there is a better way to live your life. Don't take revenge into your own hands, no matter how badly you have been hurt. If someone punches you, resist the urge to hit back. Let them punch you again if they want. And if someone sues you for your shirt, give them your jacket as well. If you are made to work an hour of overtime without extra pay, work two hours without complaining.

Always give to people who want something from you. And never refuse to lend to someone who asks.

Love Your Enemies

It is normal for people to love their family and friends while they justify hating their enemies. But there is a better way to live your life: Love your enemies! Instead of reminding yourself why you hate them, find every way possible to help them because this will make you a true child of God.

If you only show love to those who love you, how are you any different? Even criminals and terrorists love their friends and families.

Don't expect to be rewarded if this is how you love. Instead, be more like God who is kind to ungrateful people and helps those who hate him.

Service in Secret

When you do something good, don't show it off in front of everyone. Don't post it online. If you do, you will receive the temporary admiration of your followers but no reward from God.

Rather do your service to others in secret so that not even your left hand knows what your right hand is doing. God will see everything that you have done, and he will make sure that you are richly rewarded, far beyond what you have sacrificed.

Prayer

The same goes for prayer: Don't be like those hypocrites who say long, loud prayers in church. It's better to pray alone so that you can talk with your Loving Father in private. God already knows what you need even before you ask. He knows your thoughts even before they are spoken.

This is an example of how you could pray:
'My loving Father in heaven,
Everything about you is perfect and holy.
Your authority and your plans will be a reality on Earth.
Please meet my daily needs.
Please forgive me for my mistakes in the same way that I forgive others.
And guide me away from bad temptations.'

Persistence

When you pray to God for something, he will answer you.

Imagine for a moment you have a guest who arrives at your house late at night and you have no food to offer them. So, you go to your friendly neighbor and ring the doorbell, over and over until, eventually, he gets up to help you.

Think about how parents respond to their kids when they ask for something. If your son asked you for some pizza, would you give him a brick instead? Or if your daughter asked for ice cream, would you surprise her with a scorpion? Of course not! Parents aren't perfect but they know what is good for their children. And God, our loving Father, will give us good things when we ask for them.

He will even give you his beautiful spirit as a gift. But only if you ask.

Wealth

A person's value isn't measured by their bank account or the size of their house. So why do people work so hard to finance big mortgages and bank accounts? Houses can burn down, and money can be stolen. So, wouldn't it be better to invest your efforts in something that lasts forever?

I read about a man who worked many years and then sold his business for billions of dollars. He took the money and invested it through a complex legal structure to protect his assets. After he had setup this secure financial structure, God woke him up at night and said to him, "You idiot! You are going to die tonight. Who is going to enjoy all the money you tried to protect?"

It is stupid to invest everything here on Earth without investing in your relationship with God, which is going to last forever.

Loyalty

If you want to know what someone values in their life, you just need to look at what they spend their time and money on. No one can be dedicated to God and to money. It's like trying to work for two bosses at the same time - you will love one and hate the other.

Anxiety

Don't worry so much about the future. Many people stress over what they will wear and where they will live.

Look at how birds live. They don't invest in education, and they don't spend years building a career. And yet God gives them what they need to live fully. Fish have more beautiful homes in the coral reefs than the richest people in Beverley Hills. And surely people are more important to God than birds or fish!

Ungodly people obsess over material things and spend their lives working to increase their possessions. But how does this solve their problems? Can they increase their life expectancy? This would be easy for God to do so why do people stress about future wealth? Instead, if people prioritized God, he would make sure that they have everything they need to live a satisfying and fulfilled life.

Let the future worry about itself. Every day has enough problems of its own.

The Golden Rule

Always treat others how you want to be treated. This simple statement summarizes the core message of the Bible.

Teaching

My purpose is to reveal what it really means to follow the teachings of the Bible, not to change any part of it. Anybody who neglects even a small part of the Bible, and teaches others to do the same, will be the biggest loser in God's country. Those who apply the Bible's teachings to their life, encouraging others to do the same, will be very highly regarded.

Application

After watching these videos, I expect you to apply them to your life. Don't be like a lazy engineer who fails to put in deep foundations for a tall building. At first, it will seem that the new building is solid, until the day an earthquake brings it all crashing down.

Instead, you should apply these lessons and build deep foundations for your life. Then you will be able to withstand any disaster, like the greatest skyscrapers built on solid foundations, set deep into the bedrock.

4. GOD'S COUNTRY

Give Them to Me

We left California for many reasons. The death threats against Joe were becoming more frequent and the negative environment there made it increasingly difficult to keep working. More importantly, Joe believed it was time to "hit the campaign trail" and go east. So, we hired a bus and started our road trip across the states.

We tried to leave unnoticed but by the time we reached Las Vegas, there were hundreds of cars following us, hoping to get a chance to see Joe. He felt sorry for them and so we stopped near a large open field. As the crowds started to swarm around Joe, we began to set up, instructing everyone to form groups and assigning them their areas to sit down and wait.

Joe then moved through the groups and treated everyone who was sick (some people had even been dragged out of nearby hospitals) until late in the evening.

We suggested that Joe stop and send everyone home so that they could get some food. Instead, He told us to organize food for them. We started arguing about the cost of feeding five thousand people when Joe asked, "How much food do we have right now?"
I thought it was a joke, but someone said, "There is a kid who offered to share his food. He brought two burgers and two packets of fries."
"Ok. Give them to me. I'll say grace and then you can start passing out the food."
Joe prayed over the burgers and fries, then started splitting them as we passed around. Somehow, the burgers and fries kept multiplying until everyone was fed. We even collected twelve bags of leftovers.

The Venture Capitalist

After the crowd ate, Joe took a microphone and began to teach them about God through stories.

"A venture capitalist invested into many startups. The first startup had its money stolen through a scam. The second startup grew initially but, since the business had weak fundamentals, it soon failed. The third startup was well placed in a good market and it grew quickly. However, competitors also entered this market and squeezed their profit margins so hard that it also failed. The fourth startup was in a fertile market without direct competitors. It was able to grow quickly and sustainably, producing returns of sixty to a hundred times more than had initially been invested."

We asked Joe why he used stories instead of preaching about the principles more literally. He explained that people generally didn't understand the deep truths of God and needed stories to help them understand. Unfortunately, most people were so cynical that they were deaf to his message.

"Let me explain the story of the Venture Capitalist," Joe told the crowd. "When a person hears the message about God and someone "steals" this understanding from them, it's as if the investment is stolen from the person's heart. This is the first startup in which criminals stole the investment before it had any impact on the business.

The second startup with weak fundamentals is like a person who hears about God and receives it happily, but their belief is based on weak spiritual fundamentals. When life gets tough, their spiritual growth stops and fails. The startup is like a person who receives the message, and their faith grows well for a while. But eventually it is suffocated by competing priorities in their life, where ungodly things like wealth, security and status become more important to them.

In the end, the startup that succeeded is like the person who hears about God and becomes deeply and sustainably transformed. This person produces a profit for God that is sixty or even a hundred times what was originally invested."

The Network

"Here's another story that explains what God's country is like. There was a manager whose office network was hacked, and a virus spread among many of the company's computers. The IT guy explained, 'We can't be 100% sure which computers are infected. We could target those that are likely infected and wipe their hard drives immediately. That's the safe option.' The manager answered, 'That would mean taking some healthy computers offline too. We have a major deadline coming up tomorrow evening, so I want you to conduct a full diagnostic while we are working and only wipe the infected computers at the end of the project.'"

The Embryo

Joe gave another example, saying, "God's country can be thought of as a human embryo. At first it is only made up of one cell and is so small you need a microscope to see it. Over time it develops and grows into a spectacularly complex human being, made up of millions and millions of cells, able to do incredible things, even taking care of other humans."

The Network Explained

After we had left, Joe explained the story of the computer network and the virus in more detail.

"The manager who set up the computers and network is like God. The network is the world in which we live, the virus is like the agents of evil and the hacker is Satan. The IT guy is like an angel of God and the project deadline is the end of time or Judgment Day. So, just as the virus will eventually be wiped out at the end of time, people who are guilty of doing evil things will be thrown out of God's country by the angels. The healthy computers are those people who remain."

Commitment

"God's country is like a new technology discovered by a scientist. She keeps it a secret, sells everything, and invests it all into the patent and startup.

God's country is also like a spectacular work of art that is discovered by a collector who sells everything he owns to buy it.

Think about how we regularly clean out our refrigerators. There is always some food beginning to go bad. We keep the good food and throw the bad food away."

Junk Food

As we continued on our road trip, Joe complained about the junk food politicians and church leaders feed to their people. We first thought he was disappointed because we forgot to bring the leftovers with us. This confusion frustrated Joe, "How can you still be so ignorant? I'm talking about the health of our churches and country, not the leftover burgers. Our leaders serve up junk food that makes them look good but lacks true substance."

A Sign

When we arrived at our next stop, the local church leaders were waiting for us. They wanted to know whether the rumors were true and demanded Joe to perform a miracle for them as proof that he was from God.

Joe said to them, "You can read road signs, can't you? Then why can't you read the signs pointing to me?

Faithless people ask for miracles. I won't give you one, but I will give you another sign to look out for: I am going to destroy the church! And rebuild it in three days!"

5. FULFILLMENT

Legion

We stopped for breakfast at a diner where a madman started shouting at us from the parking lot. The locals tried to get rid of him and told us that he lived in the town's sewer system. They believed a demon possessed him and turned him into an animal. He was so strong that even ten cops failed to pin him down to try arrest him, only for him to escape go even deeper into the sewers.

As we left the diner, the madman kept shouting, "What do you want from me? Son of God! What are you doing here? I beg you! Don't hurt me!"
Joe walked up and asked, "What is your name?"
A strange voice from inside the man replied, "My name is Legion. I lead an army of demons. Please,

don't torture us. Let us enter another body. Don't send us into the desert!"

Joe let the demons come out of the man and they entered some animals in a nearby apartment block. Seconds later, cats and dogs began leaping through windows and jumped from balconies to their death. The madman, however, was completely healed and normal again.

The locals were so shocked that they begged Joe to leave town as soon as possible.

The Suit

At our next stop we visited Mark, a family friend of Joe. Mark, a tailor, spent hours tailoring a beautiful suit for Joe with the finest materials. At the time, we all felt it was a waste of money, an unnecessary luxury.

Joe was invited to lunch by the local church pastor, and Joe brought Mark with him. Mark was gay and his presence in the pastor's house was less than welcome. Joe asked the pastor a question in the form of a story.

"There were two gentlemen who were in debt to a banker. One owed a thousand dollars and the other owed fifty thousand dollars. During the financial

crisis, both men lost their jobs and were unable to repay their debt. Instead of foreclosing their houses, the banker decided to write off their debts. Which one would be more grateful for the debt relief?"
The pastor replied, "The one who owed more."
"Exactly. In Mark's case, he has been very kind to me. He has made me the most beautiful suit I will ever own. And while he was taking my measurements, he kissed my hands and my feet. I have forgiven his debts because he believes in me. And that is why he loves me. His sacrifice will always be remembered."

Priorities

Afterward, we visited Mark's siblings, Mike and Lucy's, and everyone was having a really great time, except for Mike. He felt that Lucy wasn't helping enough to host all the guests and complained that she was spending all her time with Joe.

"Please tell Lucy to do her part," Mike finally asked Joe. "It's unfair that I should do everything. Doesn't it bother you that she does nothing to help?"
"Mike, you're stressing over unimportant things. Lucy's focusing on what matters."

The Burger of Life

We had managed to avoid the crowds for several

days, but this came to an end when someone posted our location on Facebook. Within an hour, Joe's fan club was arriving, as well as the media, who had been trying to track us down since the burger feeding moment.

Joe went out and talked to them.
"Why are you following me? What are you looking for?"
The reporter asked, "What do you think people are looking for?"
"They haven't come this far simply because of some miracles they saw. They experienced something new. Something they cannot get anywhere else. They felt fulfilled for the first time in their lives," Joe answered. "They ate the burgers, and their hunger was satisfied. Now they want to know what it's all about. The kind of burger I am offering is free. You don't need to work for it. And it never goes bad, so you never need another one. The job that God has given me is to keep giving this type of food to the people who ask for it."

The reporter asked, "And what job has he given to people?"
"Their job is to put their faith in the person that God has sent to them."
"Why should we believe that God has sent you," the reporter continued, "Can you give us evidence?"

"That won't make a difference." Joe said. "God has given science as a gift to the world. The miracle that

you should focus on is the burger that God has sent from heaven for everyone to enjoy."
"Alright then, give us this 'heavenly' burger." the reporter asked.

Joe knew they still didn't understand. So, he explained more plainly. "I am that burger from heaven that satisfies. I am the burger of life!" Joe declared. "Anyone who comes to me will never be hungry again. Anyone who believes in me will never be thirsty again. Their soul will be completely fulfilled. And this isn't just for certain religious people - it's an open offer to anyone that accepts me. I will never refuse anyone. It is God's plan that whoever puts their trust in me will receive this glorious kind of life."

6. COMMITMENT

Division

When the reporter's interview went viral, it created another storm of controversy within the church and division among Joe's fans. They didn't believe Joe's claim that he was literally from God. People tweeted that they knew where he was born, and they knew his parents, so they thought he was delusional or lying to them.

Joe tweeted back, "No one can believe in me unless God leads them. Normal food nourishes your body, but you'll still die. Eat this burger of life, and you'll live forever."

One response implied that Joe was calling people to eat him, literally. "@Joe_official, what kind of psycho are you? You want people to eat your body? Are you leading a cult of cannibals?"

Joe tweeted again, "The burger of life is a metaphor. I can only be a living part of you if you bring me into your life."

This controversy, more than others, split Joe's followers. Many left and some joined opposition groups. Even among the team, we felt his statements made it very difficult for people to believe him.

"Why does it disturb you when I say these things? What if I started levitating and flew back up to heaven right now? Would that make you believe? Science is meaningless without God. It is the spiritual things that really matter."

Joe asked us, "Are you going to stay with me?" Powell answered. "Where should we go? Who should we follow? Nobody else understands the meaning of life like you. Even though we don't fully understand, we have chosen to believe you."

"Don't be so quick to congratulate yourselves for sticking with me" Joe said. "I chose all of you. And even then, one of you is going betray me and have me murdered."

Recruitment

Right at the start of Joe's campaign, I had left Father John to join him. I also convinced my sister, Anna, who was working for a recruitment agency at the time, that it would be better to recruit people for Joe's campaign instead.

We quickly recruited a good friend, Paulette, who brought her boyfriend, Byron. She told Byron that Joe was the leader we had been waiting for. But he was skeptical, asking "Can anything good could come out of LA?"

At their first meeting, Joe told Bryan, "You are a true man of God. True to your values and true to what you say."

"You don't even know me."

Joe explained to Byron that he knew everything about him, even minor details like what he was eating when Paulette called earlier.

"How could you possibly know all that? Unless you really are sent by God," Byron realized to his amazement.

"I am going to do a lot more than that. If you stick with me, you are going to see things that will blow your mind."

Our core team grew to twelve members, including the siblings Juan and Jacqui, Theresa, Jordan, Tim, Simon and Jake (the one who conspired with Joe's killers).

The final member of the team to be recruited was Max, the former Mayor of LA.

Venturing Out

To rebuild the campaign organization after our recent losses, Joe gave each of us individual assignments to head out and recruit more volunteers.

"The potential out there is virtually limitless. Pray that God brings us more volunteers. As you travel across the States, you will be venturing out there like poodles amongst Pitbulls. But don't protect yourselves. Don't take money with you. No credit cards, no extra clothes and not even a second pair of shoes. Go directly to the places I am sending you, and you will find people who will look after you. Accept their hospitality as payment for your work. Eat and drink whatever they offer you. And pray for God to bless them.

Whenever a church welcomes you, stay with them. Heal everyone with the power and authority I am giving you. Tell them about God's country and how soon it will be a reality. If they don't accept you, give them the finger and move on to the next place. I have no sympathy for such people. If the Nazis had seen my miracles, they would have changed and followed me. It's going to be much worse for people who have seen these miracles and still refuse to believe."

The Report

Two months later, we returned and reported countless incidents where people's lives had been changed and every kind of illness cured. All this was possible because we were sent out under Joe's authority.

"Before you all get inflated egos," Joe interrupted, "just be grateful that you have valid passports to enter God's country."

Joe asked, "When you were out there, what did people say about me? Who do they think I am?"
"The media portrays you as the leader of a radical cult. Some people think you are a spiritual guru or some kind of prophet."
"And what about you?" Joe asked, "Who do you think I am?"
We were too afraid to say something until Powell blurted out, "You are God!"
"Powell, our loving Father has revealed this to you. Let me reveal something further. God is going to make you president of his new government. For the time being, we must continue our campaign. You all must keep my real identity a secret for as long as possible."

The Unknown Preacher

During our volunteer recruitment drive, Jacqui came

across a guy who was also preaching and healing people, claiming to being working on behalf of Joe.

"I stopped him," Jacqui reassured everyone.
"Why did you do that?" Joe exclaimed.
"He wasn't one of us. How can we trust him?"
Joe explained, "He can't be against us if he is playing offence for our team."

A Crossroad

Joe warned us that everyone would turn against him. "The next few months are going to be really tough for all of us."
He predicted that the church leaders, the media and powerful politicians would use every means to discredit and incriminate him.

Powell was most upset by this and argued bitterly with Joe, saying that God could never allow them to be defeated.

Joe understood Powell's motives and gave a severe warning, "Get away from me, Satan! Don't ever get in the way of my mission! Your ambitions have already put you in opposition to what God wants. I would prefer to avoid death, but I must do what God wants. This is what I was sent to do."

Joe addressed everyone, saying, "We have travelled a

long way together. And today we have arrived at an important crossroad. You need to decide now. If you're part of my team, this mission must be your top priority. You must give up everything else. If you can't commit, it's better to leave. You just won't play a role in God's country.

"Ask yourself what you value most in your life. What are you prepared to sacrifice your life for? Would you do it for a billion dollars? For fame? For power? Or are you ready to give your life to me?

"This is about choosing a long-term investment. It is going to cost you a lot now – don't underestimate it! Be careful to weigh up the costs versus the returns and rewards."

"You can spend your life working to get rich or to gain power, and when you die you will lose everything, including your soul. On the other hand, if you dedicate yourselves to me, you will have everything you need, forever. One day I will come back, and I will reward each of you for the decision that you make.

A Little Faith

Our team's new spiritual abilities were put to the test when we were asked to treat a ten-year-old boy, whose seizures often put his life in danger. Once he fell down a flight of stairs, and on another occasion, he almost fell into a swimming pool. His mother had taken him to the best medical specialists without success and once she heard about Joe, she came in search of us. We all failed miserably despite repeated attempts to treat him.

Joe was disappointed with us. "How much longer must I have to put up with this lack of faith?"

Joe spoke for a while with the boy's mother.
"I'm afraid he is going to hurt himself when I am not there," she said. "Please help us if you can."

"If you can?" asked Joe. "Anything is possible for someone with faith."
She cried, "I have a little bit of faith. Please help me to have more."

He called the boy over and immediately he was thrown into a fit. As he writhed about on the floor, a spirit inside him screamed violently. Joe commanded the spirit to be silent and to leave the boy's body. Immediately he stopped shaking and calmed down completely. Since that day he has never had a seizure again.

Later we asked Joe why we were unable to help the boy.
"You can only force out that kind of spirit with prayer," Joe explained. "And you don't have enough

faith. You really don't need a huge amount of faith to do seemingly impossible things. If your faith was the size of an atom, you would be able pick this building up and put it down in another street. Everything is possible if you have enough faith."

For or Against

Someone posted a clip of Joe exorcising the spirit from the boy, suggesting in the video that Joe was a Satanist because he had power over demonic spirits.

Joe posted a response video, saying "It's not logical that I am working for evil. If the captain of a football team started playing against his own team, there would be chaos, and they would lose the game. How can enemies cooperate? There is no way I can be both for and against evil at same time."

"Explain to me how priests perform exorcisms? What power are they calling on? The answer is simple: I am working with God's power to fight evil."

"You need to understand this about evil spirits: When an oppressive spirit is forced out someone, it roams the streets looking for a new home. If it doesn't find another body it will eventually go back to its previous host and bring with it a whole gang of other roaming demons, making things far worse than before. This generation is in the same position."

7. PREPARATION

Father John

"He will be arriving any day now. We must prepare ourselves for Him! Everything will be made new through Him."

That was the core of Father John's message that he preached from his small church in the high desert of California, far away from the mainstream corruption of Los Angeles. He had become an outcast over the years for his predictions that God would send our country a new leader, one who would transform the church and the country, showing us a better way. Father John lived and dressed modestly and yet he had a following of tens of millions of people. People of all backgrounds and levels came to him for advice. Tens of thousands attended his gatherings. Some would fly across the country just to consult with him. Some stayed and worked for him, leaving their past life behind to join his mission – that is how I came to join Father John a few years before I joined Joe.

People would ask him, "What should we do with our lives? How can we live in a meaningful and fulfilling way?" John gave straightforward answers, "If you happen to have two cars, give one to someone who has none. If you have extra money, give it to someone who needs it."

Politicians asked him how to govern fairly. "Don't tax more than you need to," became his standard answer. Even gang leaders asked him how to take better care of their neighborhoods.

There was one group of people, however, that got his special attention: megachurch leaders. Every time they came to his meetings, he would shout, "Who warned you that God is pissed off with you? You evil snakes! Practice what you preach and stop claiming you are specially chosen by God!"

As Father John's influence grew, people speculated as to whether he was more than just an enlightened spiritual leader. Some wondered whether he might in fact be the new leader that we were expecting. Whenever pressed for an answer, he spoke emotionally of the Perfect Soul that would soon be arriving to change the world. "He is already living among us. I am so unimportant in comparison that I have no right to shake his hand. My role is simply to prepare you and point you towards him. I am preparing you through a baptism with water, but it is nothing compared to his spiritual baptism by fire. He is going to reveal himself soon. You won't have an excuse for missing it."

Baptism

On the appointed day, Joe arrived to be baptized by Father John. As he came up out of the water, the sky seemed to open, and the Holy Spirit came down on Joe. This was the sign that Father John had been waiting for.

"He's here! He's arrived! This is the one who comes after me, and yet is before me."

While He is Still Around

Over a year later, while we were campaigning, the news broke that Father John had been arrested. He had revealed the corrupt activities of powerful politicians and now they were taking their revenge.

For a while, Father John's team joined us and soon realized that we did things differently. We ate well and were known to enjoy a good party every now and then, which seemed to conflict with Father John's vow of poverty.

They confronted Joe, asking why we didn't fast and pray as diligently as they did.
Joe answered, "When a group of friends throws a farewell party for one of them, would you judge them while they celebrate? After their friend leaves, they will be very sad. But while he's still with them, they will enjoy every moment together."
"There is a deeper truth to understand. You don't fill up an electric car with gas. You don't play a vinyl record with Spotify. New tech isn't compatible with old tech. But people still love the old ways."

Evidence

Father John's team had doubts whether Joe really was the one that had been promised.

"Should we be expecting someone else?" they asked Joe directly.
"Tell him what you've seen me doing," Joe responded. "I have given hearing to the deaf, and sight to the blind. Paraplegics walk, and people with terminal illnesses are cured. And the most important thing is that the great news about God's love is being shared with everyone. Tell him about the evidence you have seen."
After they had left, Joe said, "I know how hard it is for

people to believe in me. I am not what people expected. Nevertheless, God will reward everyone who believes in me despite the offence that I cause."

8. FIRST AND LAST

The Greatest

The news about John's death in prison shocked us to the core. Rumors circulated that he had been assassinated by his powerful enemies. It made us anxious about our own situation. Joe made a speech at Father John's memorial service.

"Why did people come from all over the world to see Father John? It wasn't to see a fashionable or successful man. They came because he was a prophet, because he had the answers to their questions. John always spoke the truth to everyone he met. But people dismissed him.

"People thought he was crazy because of his clothes and lifestyle. He fasted and never drank. But they criticize me for dressing well and enjoying a drink with friends. I get canceled because my friends come from all walks of life.

"It's like rock band complaining about their fans, saying, 'When we play metal you don't headbang. And when we play hip-hop, you don't dance.' Nevertheless, wisdom is proven by its outcomes.

"John was more than just a prophet. He is greater than any human that has ever lived. He is the most important person in the country of God, quite the opposite of those who are considered VIPs today – they are the least important in God's country."

Childlike

An argument developed in the team around who should lead our team, and who would be given the most important positions in God's country. Joe suspected what was going on and confronted us about it. We had just been holding back a group of kids that had suddenly swarmed around Joe. It had been a long day, but Joe demanded that we let every single kid spend time with him, even if it took all night.

Later, he taught us the lesson, "Whenever you welcome a child in my name, you implicitly welcome me. And if you welcome me, you welcome God too. You should all be more like children. If you want to be great in God's country, humble yourself like a child."

I Want to be Generous

"Let me explain how the first will be last, and the last will be first," Joe said.

"A new car factory was built and used a recruitment agency to find employees for a monthly salary of five thousand dollars.

"In the second week of production, the factory manager asked the agency to hire a few more staff. This was repeated each week as production ramped up, so that more were hired in the third and fourth week of that month.

"At the end of the month, everyone was paid a full month's salary, even those who started much later. Those who had been hired in the first week protested that it was unfair and demanded a meeting with the manager.

"At the meeting, the manager put his case forward, 'I acted within the law, and all got paid according to your contract. Take your salary and be satisfied with it. I want to be generous. Why are you so jealous?'"

Something Missing

Joe spoke about the first and last principle again, this time with one of the wealthiest women in the country. She came to ask him what she should do to get into heaven.

"Why are you asking me this?" Joe said. "God is the one who can tell you what is 'good'. Haven't you read what God has said in the Bible already? The commandments are simple: Do not murder. Be faithful to your husband or wife. Don't steal. Don't lie. Respect your mother and father. And finally, love others as much as you love yourself."
She said, "I am doing all of that. But there is still something missing."
Joe answered, "In your case, if you want to reach your full potential, sell everything you own and give it to the poor. Invest your wealth in heaven and follow me."

She left, looking depressed. Joe said, "It's incredibly hard for someone with wealth to get into the God's country. It's like someone trying to take a flight with a hundred tons of luggage."

I asked Joe, "Wealth is relative. We are wealthy compared to most people in the third world. So how is it possible for anyone to get into heaven?"
"It is impossible for people to get into heaven," Joe answered. "But if you consider God's nature then

everything is possible."

Upset by this, Powell said. "We have given up everything for you! I left my business and a new apartment. I had such a good life, and I threw it all away to work for you. What for?"

"Trust me when I say this," Joe answered. "When I am sitting in the seat of power in God's country, you will all be senators! Anyone who gives up something precious to follow me will receive a reward that is many times more than what they gave up. And they will receive the gift of a perfect eternal life."

"But don't fool yourselves! It's not going to work out as some might expect. Many who are first now, will be last in the end. And many that are last now, will be first in the end."

Who is My Neighbor?

A professor of theology asked a similar question to test Joe's theology. He asked Joe the standard question, "What must I do to get into heaven?"
Joe replied, "What does the Bible say?"
"That we must love God with all our heart, soul and mind. And that we must love our neighbor as much as we love ourselves."

"Correct!" Joe told him. "If you do that you will live

forever and ever in heaven. Amen!"

"However," the professor continued, "Who is really my neighbor? Is it just the people living in my street? Or my community? Where does it end?"

"I will answer you with a story. One day a guy was driving through a poor suburb when he got a puncture. While he was changing the tire, gangsters beat him up, took his phone and wallet and drove off with his car. They left him bleeding to death in the gutter.

"A pastor drove by, saw someone lying on the roadside, and kept going, fearing that the criminals could still be around. A few minutes later, a regular churchgoer also noticed the man lying on the roadside, but she hoped somebody else would help him and continued driving.

"Next a Muslim man drove by and felt sorry for him. He decided he would help and stopped. The Muslim man used his first aid kit to stop the bleeding and cover his wounds. Then he lifted the beaten man into his car and drove him to the hospital where he was admitted. The Muslim man paid all the expenses, so that the beaten man could recover fully from his injuries.

"Now, which of which these three people acted as a neighbor?" Joe asked.

The professor answered, "The person who showed him mercy and compassion."
"Exactly. You should follow this example," Joe said.

9. BLINDNESS

They Don't Hate You

We had been planning to attend the biggest annual Christian conference but since Joe was receiving more death threats, it was decided that the team should attend without him.

Joe stayed nearby with his brothers (who didn't believe in him at all). They teased him that the conference would be a great opportunity to grow his brand, "Just go there and do one of your 'miracles' in front of everyone."

"It's not the right time," Joe answered. "You go. They don't hate you. People hate me because I expose their lies."

Despite this, after his brothers had left for the conference, Joe sneaked out and hid himself among the audience. People were discussing Joe amongst themselves, some saying he was good and others saying he was dangerous. Nobody spoke about him publicly because they were afraid of how the megachurch leaders would respond.

The Road Less Travelled

On the third day of the conference, out of the blue, Joe walked up onto the stage and began to speak.

"If you want a truly satisfying life, choose the road less travelled. The big highways through life are easy to drive on and most people use them. But, in the end, easy highways lead to an unsustainable and destructive life. The road less travelled will be harder to follow and only a few will ever find it. It leads to the life God wants for you."

Hypocrisy

"Watch out for hypocritical church leaders. You can follow their teachings but don't follow their example. Unless your behavior is superior to theirs, don't expect to be allowed into God's country. Hypocritical leaders are like rotten eggs - they look good on the outside but are dead and disgusting inside.

"How do you know whether someone is a hypocrite or not? Think how product reviews on Amazon work. A good product gets good reviews because it performs in the way it was advertised. If the product does not deliver what was expected, it gets bad reviews."

"You shouldn't be surprised that some supposedly 'good' Christians won't be allowed into God's country. They will send me messages, begging me to let them in, saying, 'We preached, we gave money to charity, and we went on missions! We even exorcised demons and performed miracles!' All I will say to these people is: 'I don't know you. I never knew you.'"

Politics

"To become president, you must win an election. If someone stole an election or took power by force, the people should resist that illegitimate government."

I am like an election. My people accept and follow a leader chosen by me. They don't listen to impostors who come to dominate, kill, and destroy. But I ensure that everyone will have freedom to live to their full potential."

Joe continued with another example. "I am like the ideal of a politician, someone who dedicates his life to serving their constituency. Not like those career politicians who only think about their own ambitions. Unfortunately, there are still a lot of voters who are not yet part of my constituency. My goal is to unite them so that we become a unified country under one great president.

"This is the purpose I am sacrificing my life for. And it is because of this sacrifice that the Father loves me. I am giving up my life, and later, I will take it back again, according to what my loving Father has said."

Teaching and Promise

Those hearing Joe speak were so amazed that they all wanted to find out which university or theological college he had attended, and to which church group he belonged. They wondered what the conference leaders were thinking and if they believed he was the leader that had been promised would come.

Joe said to them, "My teaching doesn't come from my own understanding. I am sharing the things that God has instructed me to teach because you are not following what is written in the Bible."

Trap Set

Joe was about to continue speaking when some megachurch leaders came up on stage and posed a question to him. They wanted to find a way to expose him and have him cancelled.

They said a member of their congregation had a secret homosexual relationship. "The church rules state that such a person should be opposed and thrown out of the church. What is your opinion?"

Joe seemed to take no notice of the question. He doodled something on a piece of paper while the seconds passed, the audience growing restless.

Joe answered, "If you want to throw someone out, it can be done by someone who has never broken a rule. So, if you are perfect, I welcome you to condemn this person right now."

Again, Joe doodled quietly while the audience watched in stunned silence. One by one, the leaders left the stage and walked out.

"It seems none of the leaders here want to throw that person out," Joe said. "Neither do I. Whoever you are, you have the freedom to be a member of the church and the responsibility to change your life and serve God."

Appearances

"I have a question to ask," Joe continued. "Why do

some of you want to kill me?"

A murmur of disbelief rumbled through the crowd. "What? Are you crazy? Who is trying to kill you?"

"People threatened my life after I said the F-word at an event. I was angry and I said 'shit' a few times to describe the real state of spiritual life in this country. That has become very controversial. But let's get some biblical perspective: the prophet Elijah murdered hundreds of people in righteous anger. Yet when I say one word in righteous anger, you want to lynch me! I wish people would stop making such superficial judgments."

A Blind Follower

That evening, after the conference had ended for the day, Joe rejoined the team. We stopped by a store, and, as we were leaving, Joe started a conversation with a blind man begging at the door. We wondered if God had caused his blindness. Was it punishment for something he had done or something his parents did? Or was it simply bad luck?

Joe answered, "It has nothing to do with guilt or punishment. He is blind so that God can demonstrate what is possible. There is still so much of God's work to do but I won't have enough time. While I'm here, I must lead by example."

Joe picked up some dirt, spat into it to make a muddy mixture which he then wiped into the blind man's eyes.
"Go and wash your face," he instructed.

While the blind man went off to wash his face, we left for our hotel. We found out later that the blind man had his sight completely restored. He was so happy that he showed himself to his friends all night long. They struggled to believe him and thought it was a practical joke, that this person was the identical twin of their blind friend. But eventually they were convinced, and they wanted to find out more.

"I didn't see him, but I know his name is Joe," said the blind man. "He put mud into my eyes and told me to wash it off. And then I could see for the first time in my life."

This started a big search for Joe all over town and it was reported to the church leaders at the conference. Of course, the leaders refused to believe it and argued that there must be some rational explanation. They cross-examined the previously blind man and his friends, even calling his parents and doctors to verify that he had been blind since birth.

The conference leaders were divided by the miracle. Some were adamant that Joe could not be sent by God because he disagreed with so much church doctrine.

Others argued that it was impossible for someone to perform so many miracles without God's help.

The conference leaders tried to convince the previously blind man that God had healed him directly. They explained that Joe is a 'sinner' and couldn't possibly have performed the miracle. He listened carefully but remained convinced, saying, "I can't judge whether Joe is a 'sinner' or not. All I know is that I was blind before I met him and now, I can see!"

They questioned him again, "Explain to us precisely what Joe did."
"Again? How many times do you need to hear it? Are you interested in becoming his followers?"

This provoked them, "Clearly you are just another employee on his payroll, just another blind follower. We trust the Bible. Joe is not to be trusted! No one even knows where he is from or who he really is."

"Wow, that's amazing," the previously blind man remarked. "You are the leaders, and you don't have a clue who performed this incredible miracle. You say that God doesn't listen to 'sinners', but even with today's medical technology, nobody can give someone their sight back when they were born blind. Joe must have done this with some greater power. It's obvious, isn't it? God listens to people who respect him and believe in him. That is something that even I understand."

The leaders had security throw him out and banned him from ever coming back, citing his sinful attitude toward church leadership and disrespect for doctrine as grounds for his expulsion.

Joe heard about the interrogation and went to find the previously blind man.
He asked him, "Do you believe that the guy who restored your sight is sent by God?"
The man asked, "Do you know who he is?"
Joe answered, "You are looking at him."
"Wow! Yes! I believe in you!" shouted the man as he bent down and kissed Joe's feet.

For and Against

The controversy regarding the healing spread quickly at the conference and stirred up passionate arguments. Everyone wondered what the conference leaders believed about Joe. If they didn't trust him, then why hadn't they stopped him or banned him already?

They wondered whether Joe was the leader they had been promised. And if it wasn't Joe, then why not? What were they expecting? Would the true leader do more miracles than Joe?

Still, most people dismissed Joe because of his

unimpressive background. And there was a growing faction of people that were openly hostile towards him. They stirred up rumors that he was planning to destroy the church and was organizing domestic terror cells to attack targets inside the US.

Father and Son

It was into this storm of expectations and fears that Joe arrived at the conference on the final morning when he took center stage.

"I am the GPS of the world," was Joe's opening line. "Whoever follows me will never be lost. They will have the coordinates to life."

"I have come to be a judge of humanity. People who are blind will be given their sight. And those that can see will be made blind."

One leader challenged Joe. "Are you suggesting that we are blind?"

Joe answered, "If you were blind, you would not be guilty. But you claim to know the truth. So, you are not blind. Therefore, you are guilty."

"How can you make such sweeping statements?" he protested. "What gives you the right to say that?"

Joe answered, "You are judging me by human standards. I don't judge you in the same way. Whatever I have said so far is true and is backed up my Loving Father who sent me. If this was a court of law, my testimony would be considered valid since it is backed up by a credible witness. My witness is the Loving Father."

"Where is your father?" someone asked.

"If you really knew who I was then you would already know who my father is," Joe answered.

He continued, "I'm not going to be around much longer. You will look for me, but you won't find me."

People wondered why they would not be able to find him. Was he going to disappear or 'go underground'? Or was it more abstract, that he would be leaving this world. Some would later use these statements as evidence he was planning to be a suicide bomber.

"You cannot follow me to where I am going because you are from this world. I am from another world. You are going to die in this broken world if you do not believe that I am who I claim to be."

"Who are you claiming to be?" someone shouted.

"All along I have been saying the same thing to you, but you still don't understand. Even after everything I have done, you still don't get it. It's because you are not part of my constituency. My people know me and follow me. And I am going to enable them to live forever. In the end you will understand that I am who I claim to be. I have done everything that my Loving Father taught me so that I will make him happy."

He said to those people who already believed him, "If you live as I have taught you, then you will be counted as one of my followers. You will know what is true and this will give you the freedom you are searching for."

"Freedom? From what?" someone asked. "We live in a free country. What freedom do we lack?"
"You are slaves of your own desires. They control you and they separate you from God. I can set you free from this kind of slavery and oppression."

Joe continued, "This doesn't change the fact that there are people here who claim to be followers of the Bible and yet, at the same time, they are planning to destroy me."

"We are followers of the Bible! What are you implying?" they shouted.

"If you were true followers, you would do the things that the Bible tells you to do. You wouldn't be filled with hate. You wouldn't think about murdering me when you hear me speaking the truth. But this is to be expected. Your forefathers in the church have done the same thing for centuries."

"Our Father is God!" they protested. "There is no one else!"

"Well, if God was your Father, then you would love me because I come from God. God has personally sent me to you. Does that make it clearer for you who I am? Since you hate me, you can't possibly be children of God. You are more like the children of Satan."

At this point the crowd became aggressive.
"Am I wrong?" Joe shouted above the noise. "Who can prove that I am guilty of something? Have I done anything wrong in my life?"

This incited a part of the crowd who erupted with violent shouts and accusations against Joe. Some said he was a heretic or a servant of Islam, a terrorist, a demon or something worse.

Joe shouted, "I am not a heretic! Nor a follower of another god! I am telling you the truth. I have the power to give my followers eternal life – they will never die!"

"Now we know you are a heretic!" they shouted. "All great men of the Bible died, even the prophets and the disciples. Are you holier than them? Who do you think you are?"

"Haven't I made it clear enough to you already?" Joe shouted back. "You are forcing me to say something publicly that I really don't want to. You will think I am trying to elevate myself. Yes, it is true what you have said. I am greater than all the prophets and disciples of the Bible. I know this because I have met them."

"Impossible! Those people lived centuries ago. How could you possibly know them?"

"Listen!" Joe said. "This is the truth about me. I existed before any human being was born."

The agitators in the crowd started hurling bottles and other objects. Joe ducked them but stood his ground and shouted above the noise, "I have done so many good things for you! Which one of these are you attacking me for?"
"We don't care about anything you have done!" they shouted. "We are angry because of what you have said. You are a normal sinful man who is claiming to be God!"
"If I am not doing God's work," Joe continued in vain, "then you can ignore me. But since I am doing great things for God, you cannot ignore the fact that I am in God and that God is in me."

Escape

The leaders at the conference instructed security to

arrest Joe. As the security guards moved closer, Joe made his final attempt to convince the crowd. "If you are running low on the fuel of life, come to me and fill up! If you have faith in me, ever-renewable energy will be given to you, energy that will regenerate itself and overflow from inside you."

Joe ran out the back and disappeared. The guards didn't chase, which landed them in trouble.
"We gave you orders to arrest him. Why did you let him get away?"
"We just couldn't do it," the guards answered. "We have never heard anyone speak so powerfully before."
"Are you also under his spell? None of the leaders has fallen for his tricks. As usual, it's the uneducated who are easily brainwashed. You fools will be damned to hell with him."

There was one church leader that tried to approach the situation differently, recommending restraint. Unfortunately, they turned on him, accusing him of being one of Joe's agents. "How can you believe that a mechanic without any theological education could become the leader of the church in this country? It is unbiblical," they concluded.

10. EVIDENCE

Facing Death

When Joe got the call, we could tell it was bad news. Mark informed us that Lucy had a terrible fever and was in ICU. They wanted Joe to come back as soon as possible. Although Joe really cared deeply about Lucy, he told Mark that we couldn't come right away.

“She's not going to die,” Joe said to us. “This is happening so that God can be recognized for his power. She is going to be in a deep sleep and in a couple of days we will go there and wake her up.”

“Is that really a smart thing to do, Joe? People up there were ready to lynch you just a few weeks ago,” we argued. “The doctors will treat her. Is it worth taking the risk?”

"What are you worried about? Don't you think I know what I'm doing? I am the GPS of life, remember?"

"Fine. We understand. But if you go, then we will come with you," said Theresa morosely. "At least when we are murdered, we will be martyrs with you."

A few days later, as we were preparing to leave, a call came to through with the shocking news that Lucy had died, and that the funeral would be held the next day.

"I'm glad this has happened," Joe said. "This is for your sakes. I am glad I wasn't there to stop it. Now, you will finally trust me."

Seeing Power

We arrived two days after the funeral. Mike greeted us but Mark refused to come out.
"If only you had taken a flight as soon as I called," Mike said, "then Lucy wouldn't have died. Nothing is impossible when you are around. I'm glad you came but it's too late."

Joe said to him, "Don't worry, your sister will live again."
"I know," Mike said, "In heaven. She has eternal life in heaven."
"I am the one that gives people eternal life. Anyone

that trusts in me will live forever and never really die. Do you believe this about me?"

"Yes. I have always believed that you are from God. You are the leader we have all been waiting for."

Mike went back inside and told Mark that Joe was waiting for him. Mark was crying as he came out. "Why didn't you come sooner? Don't you care? If you had been here, Lucy wouldn't have died!"

Joe began to cry as well. "Show me where she is buried."

They drove to the graveyard and showed Joe the grave.
"Get the coffin out and open it," Joe instructed.
"Are you mad? She's dead! She will have started to decompose. Have some respect!" Mike shouted.
"Didn't I just explain to you that you would see God's power in action? Do you trust me?" Joe said.

While they dug out the coffin, Joe prayed out loud to God, "Father, I am praying out loud so that everyone can hear what I am saying, so that they will believe it is you who hired me to do this job." Joe continued praying like this, for God's power to be demonstrated.

The coffin was removed and laid down in front of Joe. He spoke loudly, "Lucy! Wake up! Get out of the coffin!"

Almost immediately there were sounds coming from inside the coffin and a few seconds later, the lid of the coffin was kicked open. Lucy sat upright and looked at us, still dressed in her funeral clothes and holding a small bouquet of flowers in her hands.

Existential Threat

The whole thing had been captured on a few phones and it went viral in minutes. Soon every major news network was interviewing friends who had attended the funeral and the doctors who had signed her death certificate, confirming that she had been dead.

Millions of people saw what had happened and so Joe could no longer be ignored. An alliance of the country's mainstream church leaders, government officials and some powerful politicians held an emergency meeting. This powerful alliance knew that this event would lead to a massive surge in Joe's popularity, giving him influence and power at a critical time. They assumed he could use this power to divide churches and the nation, even influencing the upcoming presidential election. They knew they needed to act quickly and decisively.

"If we don't stop him now, he will recruit more radical supporters and we will lose control. Then he will be a major threat to our institutions and the government. What can be done?"

The head of the alliance stated his position. "We must not be naive. It is better for one person to be sacrificed than for the country to destroy itself."

The council voted to take strong action and to coordinate their efforts between various government departments and the church. They immediately ordered the assassination of Lucy to stop her from campaigning for Joe. She was made to disappear, but since Joe was taking precautions and surrounded by crowds in public, they couldn't easily assassinate him.

So, they devised a plan first to discredit him by framing him as a terrorist. Then they would arrest him discreetly, take him through a special court and have him quietly executed to reduce the chance of uncontrolled protests. Thanks to anti-terrorism laws, the government had the power to make this happen according to their plan.

Joe knew this would happen, so he went into hiding for some time. He stayed away from cities and avoided all digital communication and electronic payment. But the elections were approaching, and everyone expected Joe would soon make his move.

11. PRESIDENTIAL

Welcome to the Capitol

Nobody could have imagined there would be such a spectacular response to Joe's arrival in Washington.

As soon as word spread, the city came to a standstill, and hundreds of thousands of fans lined the streets with banners saying, "Joe for President" and "God is among us".

And when he finally did appear, he was riding a bicycle, making the crowds even more hysterical as he passed the White House and Capitol Hill. They chanted, "Joe for President! Joe for President!"

The Interview: Part 1

Once again, Joe was a viral sensation with videos of his spectacular arrival getting millions of views across the globe. He was invited to a special podcast with the legendary podcaster, Lex Rogan. Here is an excerpt of the discussion.

Lex: Our special guest today is the man of the hour. Joe first gained prominence in California as an associate of the now-controversial Father John. Since then, he's gained a following of millions, with some even suggesting he should be president. Joe, welcome to the podcast.

Joe: Thank you, Lex. I look forward to sharing my thoughts.

Lex: Before we get started, let me introduce our other guests for today. First up is Helen Francis, a professor of Theology at Harvard and an author of many books about the Bible. Our second guest is the well-known church leader, Pastor Jack Holmes, who leads one of the biggest churches in the country. Welcome to you both. Joe, you made quite an entrance into Washington today. What did you make of it?

Joe: I was surprised by the crowds. We didn't

organize anything. It happened spontaneously because at a grassroots level, people are tired of the traditional leadership in this country.

Jack: Did you see what they were saying about you on their banners? That's really dangerous stuff. What would happen if they acted on those statements? They could have overwhelmed the White House or Capitol Hill. Why didn't you put a stop to it?

Joe: That would be pointless. If I told them to stop, others would take over from them. It's impossible to stop this movement.

Lex: How did you manage to get this far. Who is funding this? Who is backing you?

Joe: I'm neither a Democrat nor a Republican. Nor am I funded by Russia or China. But I'm only going to answer your question if your guests will answer my question: Who was behind the success of Father John? Where did his power come from?

Helen: I don't know enough about Father John to comment. He certainly was an unusual leader, but I don't have an informed opinion.

Jack: That is a trick question. If we say that John was a self-made man, then we would be on the side with those who argue that he was really a conman. The alternative is that Father John was a prophet, that he was sent by God.

Lex: So, why is it a trick question?

Jack: It puts us in a difficult position. If we say he was faking it, we will be very unpopular. But if we believed that Father John was a prophet, then we should have listened to him. He was very influential, but also very controversial. So, the churches distanced themselves from his ministry.

Lex: Well, what is your personal view, what do you believe?

Jack: I can't give you an answer. I'm sorry, I must pass on this question.

Joe: Well, if you are not willing to answer my question, then why should I answer yours? But let me comment on what Jack just said. He said that most churches ignored John's message. And that is the key point. If you were to ask your children to tidy their rooms and your son says to you, 'Sure Dad, I will do it later,' but he never actually does it. And then your daughter says, 'No, I'm busy' but later changes her mind and does tidy her room. Which child actually listened?

Lex: Obviously the daughter listened.

Joe: Correct. And this is why many people will be in heaven who you don't expect to be there. In heaven there will be gangsters, pornstars and homosexuals because they listened. They listened to people like John and applied his message to their lives. But most people who heard John's message rejected him and his message from God. Many of them are not going to be allowed into heaven.

The Interview: Part 2

Joe: I have another example. This story involves a wealthy woman who started a new restaurant. She purchased everything that was needed and hired managers for the business. At the end of the year, she expected to make a profit, but the managers reported a significant loss. She hired accountants to perform an independent audit of the business. Unfortunately, the restaurant managers withheld information from the accountants and even threatened them. Then the investor hired lawyers to get the information, but they also received death threats and dropped the case. So, the investor sent her own daughter to negotiate with the managers in good faith. They saw this as an opportunity to intimidate the investor and hired some thugs to assault the daughter. Tragically, she died from the beating. Now, what do you think the investor did next?

Helen: Did she hire some thugs of her own?

Jack: Or she could also just move on. Replace the managers with someone better?

Joe: Correct. You understand this story well, though you don't understand who it applies to. There is a verse in the Bible that says, 'The brick that the builders rejected turned out to be the most important in the entire building.' This is precisely what has happened today.

The Interview: Part 3

Jack: Joe, I would love to know your opinion on the next president of our country. Are Christians allowed to vote for a president who is not a Christian?

Joe: Our constitution allows everyone to vote for any candidate they want. It's a matter that falls under the jurisdiction of the constitution.

Lex: That's not what Jack was expecting you to say. Helen, do you have a question for Joe.

Helen: What would you say is the key message of the Bible for today's society?

Joe: The most important principle from the Bible is that you must love God with everything you have. And the next most important principle is that you must love others as much as you love yourself. Everything that God requires can be summed up by those two principles.

The Interview: Part 4

Lex: Joe, what is on your mind?

Joe: The leaders of the church and the bible scholars claim to be authorities on the Bible. Christians should follow what they say. But they should never follow what they do! Most leaders come up with so many rules on how to be holy while they refuse to help people to follow them. There is a big surprise in store for this kind of leader.

Lex: Really? What is the surprise?

Joe: Such leaders have claimed the role of a guard at the border post, at the entrance to God's country. They claim to know who will be allowed to enter and who will not. Unfortunately, when the time comes, they themselves are not going to be allowed in! And it's not because they didn't try. They will go on missions all over the world but all they do is convert others into weak Christians, just as terrible as they are.

Jack: How dare you say that!

Joe: These leaders and scholars ignore the core meaning of the Bible. For example, they give 10% of their income to the church because the Bible says they should. But they do almost nothing to fight poverty and injustice in their own community. In fact, they generally take a hard line on people who really need a break. They claim to read the Bible every day, so how is it possible for them to be so uncaring? They are like city sewers: On the surface everything seems fine but inside they of full of shit.

Lex: I can see why you are not making many friends in high places.

Joe: That is an understatement. The church has a checkered history when it comes to dealing with dissidents. They are burned at the stake and later converted to saints. Church leaders blame their predecessors and say that they would never have executed those messengers from God. But they would have. And they are going to kill me. And they will cancel and kill my followers too. God will hold them accountable.

A Supermarket

That Sunday we went to a megachurch in Washington, led by a famous televangelist, watched by millions around the world.

Joe brought a baseball bat with him and smuggled it into the church under his coat. In the middle of the service, Joe calmly walked up onto the stage, and before anyone could stop him, he pulled out the bat and started swinging.

He took aim at anything expensive, smashing computers, projectors and sound equipment while turning over tables and throwing chairs around.

People scattered as he shouted, "Get the f*#k out of here! This is where God meets with us. But you have turned it into a f*#king supermarket!"
"Who do you think you are?" the televangelist demanded. "What gives you the right to do this?"
"I have been sent by God to deliver this message to you and to everyone else," Joe replied.
"Why should we believe you? Prove it to us that you are sent by God!"

Again, Joe refused to perform a miracle for proof. "But I will give you a sign. This sign will point to my authority. I am going to destroy the church! And after it is destroyed, I am going to rebuild it in three days!"

12. REMEMBRANCE

Precautions

Our team's last night together was the most memorable of my life.

Joe knew it was the end and although we hoped that things would turn out well, all of us knew we were in mortal danger. We took precautions to keep our safehouses a secret and only appeared in public where there were large crowds, ensuring that there were many witnesses if our opponents made a move.

Washing Clean

That night we had a real party together. After dinner, Joe collected the dirty dishes and started washing them.

"Joe, what are you doing? Let someone else wash those," said Powell, surprised.
"I'm washing the dishes myself," answered Joe.
Powell took his plate back, saying, "No way are you washing mine!"
"If you don't let me clean your dishes," Joe replied, "then you can't be a part of my team or my church."
"Really? Then why not wash my clothes and my body too?"
"That's not necessary," said Joe. "Once your plate is cleaned, you will also be clean."

Later Joe asked if we understood what he had just done for us.

"Dictators oppress their own people, and micromanagers rule the lives of their employees," said Joe, "but in my country, things are different. To be fit to lead, you must serve others. Follow my example and focus on helping each other. Students are not greater than their teachers and employees are not greater than their managers. And yet, I want you to show the utmost respect and love for other people, regardless of their position. You must love them even as much as you love yourself. If you genuinely do this, you will become known as my followers."

Performance Review

Joe spoke a lot that night about the future.

He explained he would be going away and at the end of time, the Perfect Soul would return from God to take control of the whole world, using God's army to bring every country under his control. The Perfect Soul would be given complete control and would judge everyone who ever lived.

"The Perfect Soul will separate people into two groups, just as a CEO reviews the performance of her employees, separating them into good and bad employees."

"She calls all the employees together and gives them feedback. First, she thanks the good employees for their excellent work and offers them shares in the company.

"'What did we do to deserve this?' they asked.
She answered, "When I was new to the company you welcomed me and made me feel at home. You helped me understand how the company works. When I was sick, you took on my work till I came back. And when I took a bad decision or made a mistake, you still gave me your full support. You did it without complaining and never expected to receive anything in return."
"When did we do this for you?' the good employees asked.

The CEO replied, "Every time you did it for a colleague of yours, especially the most junior colleagues, you did it for me. And that is why I am welcoming you as shareholders in my company."

For the bad employees, she only had harsh words. "None of you welcomed me nor helped me when I first joined. When I made mistakes, you criticized me and withheld your support. When I most needed your help, you did nothing."
"When did we refuse to help you?" they complained. The CEO answered, "You refused to help your colleagues, especially the junior ones. In that way you refused your help to me too. You are all fired!'"

One of You

"One of you is a traitor. One of you is planning to betray me."

We were shocked at this and argued bitterly, defending our innocence, and trying to prove our loyalty to Joe.

"I am telling you this now, so that when it actually happens, you will understand and believe me."

Finding the Way

"Listen carefully. I'm only going to be here a little while longer. And then I'm going away."
"Where are you going?" Powell asked.
"You can't come with me now," Joe answered, "but you will follow me later."
"Why can't we go with you?" Powell begged, "I'm prepared to go anywhere with you, even to prison. I'm ready to die for you!" All of us agreed with Powell.
"Are you sure? Do you know what you are saying?" Joe asked.
"Yes! I am ready to sacrifice everything," Powell replied.

Joe shook his head and replied gently, "Tomorrow you are going abandon me. It's true - I know it already. Before 9 o' clock tomorrow morning, you are going to deny that you ever supported me. And the rest of you are going to run away and hide. None of you will come to my defense."

Joe continued, "Do you remember when I sent all of you out across the country to preach and heal people? Back then I told you to go without preparation. But this time, you should make every preparation for the next phase of our mission. If you don't already have a weapon, go and buy one."

"Don't be afraid! Trust God. Trust me. Our enemies are going to accuse us of terrible crimes but that shouldn't scare you. Keep your head held high and trust in me."

"Remember that there is a reward waiting for you. You will be like a VIP guest at my father's club where we will hang out together."

Tim asked Joe, "How do we find the club? Are you going to show us the way?"

Joe replied, "You will be able to find it because you know me. Just remember the truth I have given you, to make it part of your daily life and to follow me. Then you will find the way. And when you get there, my father will let you in because we are friends. People who don't know me won't find the way. And even if they did find the club, they will not be allowed in."

Seeing God

Paulette asked, "Can't you just open our eyes so that we see God. That will be enough for us."
"Paulette, how long have we been working together? How come you still don't know who I am? You already know God because you know me. So how can you ask me to show you God? Don't you believe that God and I are one? Do you think that all these miracles were done by my own intelligence and strength? By now you should understand this."

Hardships and Corruption

"I want to warn all of you about what is going to happen before I come back. Times are going to be very rough, especially for people who trust in me."

"There are going to be wars, depressions, famines, pandemics, earthquakes and tsunamis. These are just signs that the end is beginning. The church will be under siege by enemies who want to take revenge. They will arrest you and imprison you. Some will be killed for believing in me. Although this seems terrible, I want you to consider these hardships as opportunities to share the good news about me. You don't need to prepare speeches beforehand. Just speak with the words and wisdom that my spirit will give you. And that will touch people's hearts."

"Unfortunately, many people are going to give up and follow corrupt preachers who claim to be me. If you hear anyone claiming that I have come back, don't believe them. If they claim to know when I'm coming back, ignore them. I don't even know when I will be back. Corrupt preachers will use crafty tricks disguised as miracles to convince even the most respected Christians. Remember everything I have taught you so that you won't be deceived by them. Even if thousands gather in their churches, remember that rotting corpses attract the most flies."

The Special Advisor

"After I have left, I am going to send someone special to support you so that you won't be alone. My father is going to send his special advisor to prepare you and support you on your mission. He will teach you everything you need to know and will help you to remember everything I have told you.

"If you love me, continue to do what I have asked and I will reveal everything about myself, over time."
Tim asked, "Why reveal yourself only to us and not to the whole world?"
Joe replied, "The Father and I can only come to live in the hearts of people who love us. Someone who does not love me - and therefore does not love my Father - cannot have God revealed to them."

"Don't be afraid of the future. Even though leaders are preparing their attack, I will be going to my father. So, ask me for whatever you need, and I will make sure it is done. If you love me, you would be happy that I am going."

Stay Connected

It was just past midnight and Joe wanted to pray (as he often did). So, we left the safehouse to go to a nearby park to find a quiet spot. All of us went with except for Jake, who left the group after speaking to

Joe in private.

"There is so much more I want to tell you, but time is running out. Even though I am leaving, you must stay connected to me so that you can get everything you need from God. Just like the cells in your body need to stay connected to your bloodstream to get oxygen and food. Disconnected cells will die. If you stay connected to me, your prayers will be answered, and you will bring honor to God."

As I Have Loved You

"I love all of you so much. Much more than you can imagine. My Father loves me when I do what he wants. If you keep doing what I ask, I will love you in the same way and you will be filled with joy, as much as I am filled.

"Never forget what I have taught you: love others just as I have loved you. This is demonstrated by spending your life for those you love."

No Excuse

"Our time is running out. I must tell you one more thing. You are going to be my representatives after I have left. Unfortunately, you are going to be hated because they hate me. And every crime they commit against me, they will commit against you because they are enemies of God. They will expel you from their churches and discredit you in public. Some of you will be murdered. Yet, they will say they are doing God's work.

"I have given everyone a fair chance to make their own decision whether to believe me. I have performed miracles that nobody can explain so there is no excuse to ignore God. If I had never come, then perhaps people would have felt that God was unjust because they were never given a genuine choice to believe. Nevertheless, most people will choose not to believe me and prefer to hate God instead.

"Remember everything I have told you, so that when the difficult times come, you will know I was telling the truth. Don't be afraid. God will send you his special advisor to give you peace no pastor or president can provide. The advisor will speak on my behalf, and he will bring people to an understanding that they need God in their lives. There is so much more I want to tell you. The advisor will teach you and lead you to the truth."

13. BETRAYAL

It's Time

When we reached the park after midnight, Joe asked us to guard the entrance. Then he took Powell, Jacqui, and Juan with him into the park to keep close watch while he prayed. As he reached a secluded spot, Joe fell to his knees and prayed as if his life depended on it.

Powell, Jacqui and Juan fell asleep. Joe woke them up later with stern words, "Can't you stay awake for even an hour? I need you to pray with me! Pray that you don't give in to your temptations."

Joe went back and continued to pray as passionately as before. When he came back an hour later, he found them asleep once again. This time he did not wake them up and returned for a final prayer session, praying with such intensity that by the end he was drenched in sweat.

Once he had finished, he woke them up. "It's time."

Deadly Force

Just then, Jake appeared at the park entrance and, without saying a word to us, he walked up to Joe and hugged him. His embrace wasn't a greeting. It was a goodbye. Seconds later, a heavily armed black ops team charged into the park and surrounded Joe.

We panicked and ran. Powell fired several shots before disappearing. One bullet hit a soldier in the neck, dropping him next to Joe.

"Don't shoot!" Joe shouted as he held up his hands in front of the soldiers. He leaned over the fallen soldier and touched the wound. Immediately it stopped bleeding and the soldier regained consciousness. Joe shouted so we could all hear, "People who live by violence will die by violence! I don't need your weapons! Mine are more powerful."

Joe addressed the soldiers as they arrested him, "Why are armed to the teeth? Am I dangerous? Why didn't you arrest me during the day when everyone could see what you are doing?"

They took Joe to a nearby airport and flew him to a secret location for interrogation.

Interrogation

What we know about the next few days comes from leaked documents and transcripts. They describe how Joe was interrogated using every means to extract information from him.

They asked him the same questions over and over: "Who are you? Who are you working for? Al-Qaeda? Russia? China? Who is your leader? What are your targets? Who are you?" They stripped him naked and had the guards punch and kick him while he was blindfolded. They taunted him, saying that they would stop beating him if he would prove he was from God by identifying who had hit him.

Joe never broke. He just repeated the same answers: "I haven't done anything in secret. Everything I have said and done has been in public. It's all there online. Go and look for yourself and you will know everything about me. You can even ask my enemies - they know exactly what I have been saying and doing."

Evidence was needed and so evidence was fabricated. Photographs were made and documents were forged, emails manufactured and associations to terrorist networks were developed. Deals were made with low level domestic terrorists to testify that they had planned attacks on churches and other US targets, under Joe's instructions. In exchange they were promised an early release from prison.

During the secret court proceedings, Joe refused representation and waived his right to cross-examine the witnesses. He never contested the faked evidence.

When he was put on the stand, they asked the same questions again.
"Tell us. Who are you?", asked the prosecutor.
When Joe refused to speak, he was warned that he was obliged to give an answer.
"Are you from God?" one of the judges asked directly.
"What you have said is true," Joe responded.

After brief deliberations, the guilty verdict was returned.
"This court finds the evidence sufficient to prove the defendant is guilty of planning acts of terrorism. The defendant's network is large, armed and committed to carrying out the defendant's orders. The defendant has refused to cooperate. This court concludes that the defendant is a serious and continuing threat to the security of the state. The defendant is hereby sentenced to death by lethal injection."

The Source of Power

Joe's only chance was to receive a presidential pardon.

The media stoked anger against Joe, resulting in huge protests across the country calling for his execution and for his organization to be destroyed.

The president requested an interview with Joe before making his decision.
"Are you the leader of the church?" the President asked Joe on the call.
"Is that who you think I am?" Joe replied, "Or did one of your advisors give you that information?"
"I'm not an expert on the bible. How should I know. I assume that you are a Christian leader because of who your enemies are. Why else would they go to such extremes to get rid of you?"
"Mr. President, my country is not on this earth. If it were, my followers would be rioting and starting a revolution right now,"
The president said, "So you are a leader. Are you the leader in your country?"
"I am," Joe replied. "But I have come to your country to tell people what the truth is. People who understand truth, listen to me."
"What is truth?" the president wondered.

The president discussed further with his advisors, among them some prominent Christian leaders.
"I don't think this man is guilty." the president said. "He hasn't actually committed a crime that I can be sure of."

His intelligence and security advisors disagreed with

him, reminding the president of Joe's terrorist links and his public declaration that he will destroy the church.

The Christian advisors argued from a different angle, explaining how Joe was undermining American institutions by teaching a corrupt gospel and making blasphemous claims that he was the Son of God. They argued that he was leading an insurrection to establish his vision of God's country.

The president returned to the interview even more unsure.

"Who are you, really? Where are you from, exactly?" The President asked Joe many questions, but he stayed quiet.

"Joe, why aren't you defending yourself?"

Joe remained silent.

"Talk to me. Let me help you. Give me something," the President urged. "These are serious accusations. Don't you get it? I can save your life."

"No, you can't," Joe replied. "Your power comes from your position, and that authority is given from above. The real guilt lies with those who conspired to kill me."

From this point on, the president wanted to find a way to pardon Joe, but his advisors remained unanimously opposed. They argued that public opinion of Joe had plummeted with a majority believing he was probably a terrorist. And the president's own ratings were dangerously low with his re-election campaign kicking off shortly.

His advisors saw this as an opportunity to act tough on domestic terror and regain some vital support. They suggested pardoning a well-known Christian zealot. The President protested, "That guy murdered an abortionist. Now you want me to save his life and condemn an innocent man?"
A senior advisor said, "You are expected to act in the interests of the state. At this crucial time, you are also expected to act in the interests of your party. This isn't the time to make decisions based on your own personal conscience."

The president gave up. "So, it's decided then. I want it on the record that I disagree with this course of action but followed the recommendations of my advisors. I will not be held responsible for this."

After receiving the president's decision, Joe was moved to a maximum-security facility where preparations had been made for his arrival.

14. EXECUTION

Denial

After Joe's arrest, Powell was keeping a low profile when someone on the subway recognized him and asked if he knew Joe.
"No. No I don't know him. I know who he is, but I never met him." Powell answered. He was terrified, expecting to be arrested at any moment.

Powell stopped for breakfast when a couple approached him.
"Aren't you one of the people who travelled with Joe?" they asked.
"What! Are you crazy? I have never had anything to do with Joe or his organization."

He left hurriedly in an Uber. The Uber driver noticed

Powell's agitation, asking him if he was upset about the news of Joe's arrest.
"Why is everyone so interested in this? I don't know the man. I swear that I have never met him! Mind your own damn business!"
As Powell got out of the cab, he saw that it was 9:00am and the terrible realization dawned on him.

Blood Money

The leaked documents described how difficult it had been for Joe's opponents to arrest him because of the large public crowds and the precautions his team had taken. Fortunately, the perfect solution to their problem presented itself to them.

Jake, our campaign treasurer, understood the situation and took matters into his own hands. He approached a member of the alliance and agreed to help capture Joe discreetly. For his assistance, they paid him three hundred thousand dollars.

Infamy

Joe knew precisely what Jake was doing. And yet, Joe stuck to his plan.

The night that Joe was arrested, Jake left us to make a call to his alliance contact. He informed them of the time and place where Joe could be found. He received instructions to go back to the park and identify Joe to the special ops team when they arrived. When Jake entered the park and hugged Joe, he completed the most infamous betrayal.

Regret

We don't really know why Jake chose that path. Later, perhaps overwhelmed with regret at hearing the news of Joe's death sentence, he withdrew the blood money and stormed into an alliance meeting, throwing the cash at them while shouting that Joe was innocent. They ignored him, saying he was responsible for his own actions.

Later that day, Jake took a shotgun and ended his life.

Bring Me Home

During his final hours in the park, knowing that his best friends were about to abandon him, Joe had prayed to God for us:

"Father, the time has come. If only there was another way to carry out your plan. If only it didn't have to be so painful and humiliating. Does it have to be this way? This is what you want, so I will do it. Any honor that this brings me, I will use to honor you.

"Please protect everyone that has been with me. I have taught them everything you asked me to share and that is why they are going to be targeted. They don't belong here, but we cannot take them out of this world yet. Please protect them and continue teaching them your truth so that they will be led towards perfection, which is the reason why I am sacrificing my life.

"It is sad that most people don't know you at all. But at least my team knows you since they finally believe in me. Over time, I will continue to show them more of you so that deep in their hearts they will know that you and I love them, and that we are living in them.

"And that is the way to eternal life: to know God, you and me. You have given me authority over every person so that I can give eternal life to everyone.

"I hope that everyone who believes in me will be as unified as you and I are. Then everyone will know that you have sent me and that you love them as much as you love me.

"I'm almost at the end of my mission. Please bring me home to the magnificence we had before the universe began."

It is Finished

On entering the death row, Joe was stripped naked and humiliated by the guards. They put a tie on him and bowed down, laughingly calling him "Mr. President!"

Once in his cell, a prisoner nearby taunted Joe, "Aren't you that guy that says he is a god? Brilliant! Just open these doors and get us all out of here!"
"Have some respect!", another inmate spoke in defense. "This guy is obviously innocent."
Then he said to Joe, "Please remember me when you are a president in your country."
Joe replied, "I promise you that tomorrow you will wake up in paradise."

Joe refused his last meal and not long afterwards, the guards arrived to walk him to the execution chamber. He was strapped down onto a table and shaved clean. Then the room's blinds were opened to reveal the witnesses and cameras.

Joe, speaking loudly, said, "Father, forgive them! They don't know what they're doing."

As the final preparations were being made, some witnesses hurled insults at him. "You said you would destroy the church and rebuild it in three days! Save yourself! Let us see you break out of here!"
A church leader shouted, "You were able to rescue

others. So, prove yourself! Save yourself!"

A signal was given upon which the lethal injections were administered, and Joe started to feel unbearable pain.

He cried out, "Father! God! Why have you abandoned me?"

With his last breath he declared. "It is finished."

A team of doctors examined his body and officially recorded Joe's time of death.

Aftershock

It has since become common knowledge that this 'man', if you can call him that, was unjustly convicted. And not only that, but he was innocent in the truest sense. He was, for lack of a better word, perfect.

The three years that I had spent with him brought me to the point where I could no longer hold onto my doubts about him. Even the mysteries and things I can't explain, I have come to possess as understanding.

Therefore, despite my previous doubts and arguments to the contrary, I can no longer believe anything other than this: Joe was, and is, the son of God.

And yet, together, we murdered God. We conspired to kill the perfect gift. And as if to confirm our crime, a few moments after his final words, an unprecedented earthquake struck Washington, causing a massive blackout across the city. Even Joe's prison guards, who had been so vulgar, became immediate followers when they felt the prison building shake as Joe's soul left his body.

15. END OF THE BEGINNING

An Open Grave

We were too afraid to attend Joe's funeral. From various accounts it was a quick and muted event, with an overpowering police presence and stringent security checks on mourners.

It was fortunate that Joe was even given a civilian burial, only possible thanks to an influential church leader who had been a quiet supporter of Joe. He managed to convince the authorities to bury Joe with dignity. The alliance was concerned that Joe's followers would steal his body and claim that he had risen from the dead. So, they took the ultimate precautions, heavily guarding the graveyard and placing it under high tech surveillance. As a further precaution, Joe's body was placed in a hardened steel coffin and welded shut.

Three days after the execution, at sunrise, two women came to pay their respects at Joe's quiet grave. However, upon arriving they found the grave opened and the coffin empty. They couldn't find any guards, and phoned us in total shock, crying that someone had stolen Joe's naked body and left behind his burial suit. The suit was perfectly folded and placed in the coffin.

The authorities immediately blamed us, though I don't know how we could have overpowered the guards without any casualties or detection. The leaked documents, however, showed that the guards had run away after a significant earthquake aftershock was followed by a blinding light from the grave. They were paid a huge sum of money to change their testimony and threatened if they ever told the truth.

Alive

After the two women had reported the missing body, a stranger approached them and asked what had happened.

"Our friend was buried here, but now his body is gone," they answered.
"But why are you looking for him here when he is alive?"

Suddenly, the women recognized who they were talking to. "Joe! It's you!"
Joe said, "It's so great to see you. I'd love to stay, but I must go because my father is expecting me. You mustn't hold onto me. Please go back to the team and tell them what you have seen. I am coming to visit them soon."

Perplexed

About a week after the funeral, I was taking a bus back to New York with a friend. A guy sitting next to us noticed that we were a bit depressed and started a conversation.

"What's the matter?" the stranger asked.
We answered honestly, "We are going through a tough time. We were close friends of Joe."
"I'm very sorry to hear that. Who is he?" the stranger asked.

Clearly, he didn't know anything, so we explained the whole story to him, from beginning to end. We talked about Joe's miracles, his teachings, and the tremendous hope that people had placed in him. We all thought he would be the leader the country had been expecting, someone who would bring the change that we deeply needed. We explained how things went wrong, how people turned against him after he was convicted, how they even celebrated his death.

"But now everything is upside down because his body has disappeared. It was removed from his grave and none of us knows who did it. We don't understand why all this had to happen."
"You don't know why?" the stranger asked. "How come you still don't understand?"

I was perplexed by the stranger's question and didn't know how to answer him.
"You have missed the whole point of his death," the stranger continued. "Don't you know that he had to die?"

Then the stranger explained everything to us, quoting from the Bible to demonstrate why Joe had to die for the church and how this had all been according to his plan.

We invited the stranger for dinner that evening. At one point we finally realized that the stranger was actually Joe! And, just as soon as we realized, he disappeared.

As we replayed the day's events through our minds, we knew there was something different about the stranger because his words were so rich in truth that it burned in our hearts and minds.

Forgiven

Around the same time, Powell packed his bags for California.

"I'm tired of waiting for something to happen. I'm going surfing! And I'm going back to my old job," he wrote in an email to everyone.

Several followers joined him on the beach that weekend, even though the surf was flat and after an hour of trying to catch some waves, they paddled back to shore. Just as they were coming in, someone on the beach shouted that they should try 100 yards to the south. They thought the stranger was mad, but they decided to try anyway. Two minutes later a huge set of waves began to form, and they were all perfectly positioned to catch some of the best waves of their lives.

Powell rode a massive wave right up to the shore, abandoned his board and sprinted toward the man on the beach. "It's Joe! It's got to be Joe!" he shouted to the others. Powell knew that there was only one person who had control over the laws of nature and would do something like that.

Joe had already prepared a small breakfast for their reunion. When they had finished eating, Joe turned to Powell and asked, "Do you love me?"

"Yes."

"Then take care of my followers," said Joe.

A few minutes later, Joe interrupted the conversation again and asked Powell a second time, "Do you really love me?"
Powell answered, "Yes. Of course. You know that I do."
"Look after my followers," said Joe.

Then Joe asked him a third time, "Powell, do you love me?"
Powell started crying, "Joe, you already know everything about me. You know that I would do anything for you."
"Then take care of my followers."

Joe did this to forgive Powell for each time he had denied knowing him.

Joe continued, "Powell, you'll suffer a lot because you trust me. You'll be imprisoned several times and be executed for your faith in me."
"What about the others?" Powell asked. "What's going to happen to them?"
"Don't worry about them. Why does it matter to you?" Joe said, slightly annoyed. "I could make them live until I come back. That's for me to decide. You should focus on staying true to me."

No Doubt

In the weeks following Joe's death and disappearance,

we had received almost five hundred reports of people having seen him and spoken with him. Almost everyone was convinced that Joe was alive, except for Tim, one of the original members of the team.

"I don't believe the photos. I will believe it when I see him with my own eyes," Tim complained. "I want to be able to shake his hand and poke him in the eye. Then I will be sure he is really alive."

Tim got what he wished for. We were having lunch in a safehouse when Joe suddenly appeared in the room. When Joe greeted Tim, he said, "Here is my hand. Shake it."

Tim, in shock, shook his hand after which Joe said to him, "Now you can stick your finger in my eye."
Tim broke down crying, "My God! My God! I believe you!"
"Tim, you have only believed in me because you have been lucky enough to see me in person," said Joe. "But it is better to believe in me without having proof."

Joe ate lunch with us and afterward he suddenly disappeared again.

Spread the News

Joe appeared to us one last time near Washington where he gave us his final instructions.

"Your mission is this: Go to every state and to every country and tell them the great news about me. Tell them that everyone who believes in me will be liberated from death. They will be able to do miracles, even greater miracles than I did. Remember to teach them everything I have taught you."

"Before you leave Washington," Joe warned, "wait for my spirit, the special advisor from God. He will equip you for your mission with powerful strategies and the knowledge that you need. Once he has equipped you, your job is to go out and show the whole world that I am alive."

EPILOGUE

"Who is Joe?" asked the author.

It should be clear to the reader that Joe is a reconstruction of Jesus. Jesus is the most influential figure in history, yet few people take the time to ask the question, 'Who is Jesus?'

In Jesus' time, this is the question they were asking. And it remains the key question for every individual today. Was he simply a good teacher, or something more meaningful and powerful?

The original four gospels provide the answer. Unfortunately, "modern" people today struggle to understand these ancient texts without significant studying and assistance.

Over the centuries, attempts have been made to overcome this problem by translating the text into a more accessible languages, such as English. The Gospel of Joe takes another step.

The aim of this "translation" of the original four gospels into one book is to make it readily accessible to any person living in a modern, western, urban society without the need for an interpreter or religious education. This is not a translation of words but a transplanting of the meaning into a modern-day story that everyone can understand for themselves.

This book makes no claim to improve on the original gospels, just as Tyndale's first English translation could not supersede the original Greek, Hebrew and Aramaic manuscripts. Anyone who desires to get closer to the texts, to access their deeper meaning, they must refer to the originals as much as possible.

It is undeniable that there was a man named Jesus who claimed to have done miracles, who built up a large following and was executed by the Romans at the request of local religious leaders.

He taught many lessons, many of them beautiful, many mysterious and many subversive in nature. He developed such a passionate following that his growing support threatened those in power. Even in our modern world with its laws, we know that such injustices are real.

Even after his death, those who knew him dedicated their lives to telling people about him. They followed his instructions, even when it cost them everything.

Empires have fallen and been forgotten but Jesus remains, living in the hearts of those transformed by him.

They all knew the answer to the question. Hopefully this book can help you to find your own answer.

BIBLICAL REFERENCE

1. Power

Prove It: Mt 4:1-11; Mk 1:12-13; Lk 4:1-13

Power to Save: Mt 27:1-25; Mk 15:1-15; Lk 23:1-25; Jo 18:28-19:15

I'm Not Ready: Lk 2:25-38, 47-52; Jo 2:1-11

The Senator's Son: Jo 4:43-54

Going Viral: Mt 4:23-25; Mk 1:38-39; Lk 4:14

Jealousy: Mt 13:54-58; Mk 6:1-6; Lk 4:15-30; Jo 4:44

2. Forgiveness

Forgiveness, Not Sacrifice: Mt 9:9-13; Mk 2:13-17; Lk 5: 27-32, 19:1-10

Authority to Forgive: Mt 9:2-8; Mk 2:1-12; Lk 5:17-26
Unexpected Faith: Mt 8:5-13; Lk 7:1-10
Alternative Energy: Jo 4:1-42

3. Teachings

True Happiness: Mt 5:3-12; Lk 6:20-23
Purpose: Mt 5:13-16
Anger: Mt 5:21-25; Lk 12:58-59
Lust: Mt 5:27-30
Divorce: Mt 5:31-32
Judging Others: Mt 7:1-5; Lk 6:37,41-42
Revenge: Mt 5:38-42
Love Your Enemies: Mt 5:43-48; Lk 6:27-36
Service in Secret: Mt 6:1-4; Lk 6:38
Prayer: Mt 6:5-15; Lk 11:2-4
Persistence: Mt 7:7-11; Lk 11:5-13
Wealth: Mt 6:19-20; Lk 12:13-21, 33
Loyalty: Mt 6:24; Lk 12:34
Anxiety: Mt 6:25-34; Lk 12:22-31
The Golden Rule: Mt 7:12; Lk 6:31
Teaching: Mt 5:17-20
Application: Mt 7:24-29; Lk 6:46-49

4. God's Country

Give Them to Me: Mt 14:13-21; Mk 6:30-44; Lk 9:11-17; Jo 6:1-13
The Venture Capitalist: Mt 13:1-9,18-23; Mk 4:1,14-20;

Lk 8:4,11-15
The Network: Mt 13:24-30
The Embryo: Mt 13:31-32; Mk 4:30-32
The Network Explained: Mt 13:36-43
Commitment: Mt 13:44-46
Junk Food: Mt 16:5-12; Mk 8:14-21
A Sign: Mt 16:1-4; Mk 8:11-14

5. Fulfillment

Tornado: Mt 8:23-27; Mk 4:35-41; Lk 8:23-25
Legion: Mt 8:28-34; Mk 5:1-15; Lk 8:27-35
The Suit: Mt 26:6-13; Mk 14:3-10; Lk 7:36-50; Jo 11:1-5,12:1-8
Priorities: Lk 10:38-42
The Burger of Life: Jo 6:25-51

6. Commitment

Division: Jo 6:52-71
Recruitment: Mt 10:2-4; Mk 3:16-19; Lk 5:1-11,6:13-16; Jo 1:35-51
Venturing Out: Mt 9:35-10:16; Mk 6:7-11; Lk 9:1-5,10:1-16
The Report: Mt 16:13-20; Mk 6:12-13, 8:27-30; Lk 9:6,10:17-20
The Unknown Preacher: Mk 9:38-40; Lk 9:49-50
A Crossroad: Mt 16:21-28; Mk 8:31-38; Lk 9:22-26; Jo 12:23-28

A Little Faith: Mt 17:14-21; Mk 9:14-29; Lk 9:37-42
For or Against: 12:22-45; Lk 11:14-26

7. Preparation

Father John: Mt 3:1-12; Mk 1:1-9; Lk 3:1-18; Jo 1:19-28
Baptism: Mt 3:13-17; Mk 1:9-11; Lk 3:21-22; Jo 1:29-34
While He is Still Around: Mt 9:14-17; Mk 2:18-22; Lk 3:19-20, 5:33-39
Evidence: Mt 11:2-19; Lk 7:18-23

8. First and Last

The Greatest: Mt 11:7-18, 14:1-12; Mk 6:14-29; Lk 7:24-35
Childlike: Mt 18:1-4,19:13-15; Mk 9:33-35, 10:13-16; Lk 9:46-48, 18:15-17
I Want to be Generous: Mt 20:1-16
Something Missing: Mt 19:16-30; Mk 10:17-22; Lk 18:18-23
Who is My Neighbor: Lk 10:25-37

9. Blindness

They Don't Hate You: Jo 7:2-3
The Road Less Travelled: Mt 7:13-14; Jo 7:14
Hypocrisy: Mt 7:15-23; Lk 6:43-45
Politics: Jo 10:1-21
Teaching and Promise: Jo 7:15-19
Trap Set: Jo 8:3-11

Appearances: Jo 7:19-24
A Blind Follower: Jo 9:1-38
For and Against: Jo 7:25-31, 10:19-21
Father and Son: Jo 7:33-36, 8:12-59, 9:39-41, 10:22-38
Escape: Jo 7:32, 44-53, 10:39

10. Evidence

Facing Death: Jo 11:1-16
Seeing Power: Jo 11:17-44
Existential Threat: Jo 11:45-57, 12:9-10

11. Presidential

Welcome to the Capitol: Mt 21:1-11; Mk 11:1-10; Lk 19:28-38; Jo 12:12-19
The Interview Part 1: Mt 21:23-32, Mk 11:27-33; Lk 19:39-40, 20:1-8
The Interview Part 2: Mt 21:33-46; Mk 12:1-12; Lk 20:9-18
The Interview Part 3: Mt 22:15-46; Mk 12:13-37; Lk 20:20-44
The Interview Part 4: Mt 23:1-36; 12:38-40; Lk 11:37-53, 20:45-46
A Supermarket: Mt 21:12-17; Mk 11:15-19; Lk 19:45-48; Jo 2:13-25

12. Remembrance

Washing Clean: Jo 13:1-17,34
Performance Review: Mt 25:31-46
One of You: Mt 26:20-25; Mk 14:18-21; Jo 13:18-30
Finding the Way: Mt 26:31-35; Mk 14:27-31; Lk 22:31-34; Jo 13:31-14:7
Seeing God: Jo 14:7-11
Hardships and Corruption: Mt 24:3-51; Mk 13:3-37; Lk 21:5-36
The Special Advisor: Mt 21:21-22; Jo 14:12-31
Stay Connected: Jo 13:27, 15:1-8
As I Have Loved You: Jo 15:9-17
No Excuse: Jo 15:18-16:13

13. Betrayal

It's Time: Mt 26:26-46; Mk 14:32-42; Lk 22:40-46
Deadly Force: Mt 26:47-56; Mk 14:43-50; Lk 22:47-53; Jo 18:1-11
Interrogation: Mt 26:57-66; Mk 14:53-64; Lk 22:54, 66-71; Jo 18 :12-14, 19-23
The Source of Power: Mt 27 :1-25; Mk 15 :1-15 ; Lk 23:1-25; Jo 18:28-19:15

14. Execution

Denial: Mt 26:58, 26:69-75; Mk 14:54, 14:66-72; Lk 22:54-62; Jo 18:15-18, 25-27
Blood Money: Mt 26:3-5, 14-16; Mk 14:1-2, 10-11; Lk 22:1-6; Jo 13:2

Infamy: Mt 26:47-50; Mk 14:34, 44; Lk 22:47; Jo 13:18-30, 18:2-3

Regret: Mt 27:1-10

Bring Me Home: Mt 26:36-46; Mk 14:32-42; Lk 22:39-46; Jo 17:1-26

It is Finished: Mt 27:26-50; Mk 15:16-37; Lk 23:26-46; Jo 19:16-30

Aftershock: Mt 1:18, 27:50-56; Mk 15:38-40; 1:26-38, 23:47-49

15. End of the Beginning

An Open Grave: Mt 27:57 – 28:5; Mk 15:46 - 16:4; Lk 23:53 – 24:3; Jo 19:38 – 20:10

Alive: Mt 28:5-10; Mk 16:5-7; Lk 24:4-9; Jo 20:11-18

Perplexed: Mk 16:12-13; Lk 24:13-32

Forgiven: Jo 21:1-23

No Doubt: Mk 16:14; Lk 24:36-39; Jo 20:19-29

Spread the News: Mt 28:17-20; Mk 16:19; Lk 24:50-51

www.ingramcontent.com/pod-product-compliance
Lightning Source LLC
La Vergne TN
LVHW012117170826
845678LV00014BA/2975

* 9 7 9 8 2 1 8 9 7 7 6 9 6 *